For Nina, Mark, and Julie,
Boss yourself or be bossed (who said that?)
—R.B.

To Smokey,
for all the things you haven't said
—D.C.

Henry Holt and Company, Inc.
Publishers since 1866
115 West 18th Street
New York, New York 10011

Henry Holt is a registered
trademark of Henry Holt and Company, Inc.
Text copyright © 1997 by Robert Burleigh
Illustrations copyright © 1997 by David Catrow
Published in Canada by Fitzhenry & Whiteside, Ltd.
195 Allstate Parkway, Markham, Ontario L3R 4T8.

Library of Congress Cataloging-in-Publication Data
Burleigh, Robert.
Who said that?: famous Americans speak / Robert Burleigh;
illustrations by David Catrow.
p.   cm.
Summary: A collection of quotations along with the story
behind the words and the people who voiced them.
1. Celebrities—United States—Quotations—Juvenile literature.
2. Quotations, American—Juvenile literature.   [1. Celebrities.
2. Quotations.]   I. Catrow, David, ill.   II. Title.
PN6084.C44B87   1996   081—dc20   96-19985

ISBN 0-8050-4394-2
First edition—1997
Printed in Mexico
3 5 7 9 10 8 6 4 2
The artist used pen and ink on paper to create the illustrations for this book.

WHO SAID THAT?

Famous Americans Speak

by Robert Burleigh

Illustrated by David Catrow

Henry Holt and Company • New York

CONTENTS

Introduction

Quotations can be ways to learn about people, quotations can be ways to get new information, and quotations can be just plain fun. The quotations in this book are a bit of all three.

The quotations take the reader from an early European sighting of the New World to the present—but they do not make this a history book. They are only a selection of what's lively, unusual, or deeply moving among the many lively, unusual, and deeply moving things said by famous and lesser-known people. Indeed, the list could be expanded to fill volumes.

The book is called *Who Said That?* The truth, however, is that some of the quotations are actually taken from things people wrote—in books, letters, or newspapers. But they feel so direct and they have often become so much a part of American folklore that they seem to have been uttered out loud (perhaps they were in some cases, before the person wrote them down).

All the quotations, besides being interesting in themselves, reveal something of the speaker's personality. For this very reason, we have taken the liberty of ordering the book according to themes or ideas, or more commonly, for the humor found in pairing two dissimilar personalities. For only on the pages of this book can Henry David Thoreau and Babe Ruth stand side by side!

"Tierra! Tierra!"

Such simple words. Yet the events that followed them would change the world in many ways. Gazing into the sea-black darkness on the early morning of October 12, 1492, a Spanish sailor named Rodrigo de Trianna shouted: "Land! Land!" (*Tierra* means *land* in Spanish.) Shortly thereafter, the cannon on the small ship *Pinta* boomed to alert its two companion ships that the long thirty-three-day journey across the Atlantic Ocean was over. The expedition's leader, Christopher Columbus, thought he had reached some part of Asia. In fact, he had arrived at a small island in the Bahamas: the doorway to two huge continents unknown to Europeans. Queen Isabella of Spain had offered a large reward to the first sailor to sight land. But did Rodrigo get the reward? Not one coin of it. Columbus claimed to have seen a distant light a few hours earlier, and on the strength of this, clever Chris took the cash for himself!

"Time is money."

Benjamin Franklin was not one to fritter away time. Despite the quote, however, Ben did more than just fatten his wallet (though he did that, too). He started life as a printer. Later he began publishing *Poor Richard's Almanack*. This annual book (containing health tips, weather notes, and proverbs) became an early American best-seller. In 1748, at age forty-two, Franklin had made enough money to retire—but he was just getting warmed up! He studied electricity and invented the lightning rod, he designed the famous Franklin stove, and he aided the American struggle for freedom. He helped write the Declaration of Independence as well as the American Constitution. His last public act was to sign a petition to end slavery. How's that for making use of your time? Hey—if you use *your* time and save up your dimes and quarters, you can catch Ben's wise and kindly face on a hundred dollar bill!

"The chief business of the American people is business."

Calvin Coolidge's idea of what America was about is neatly contained in the above quote. A plain-living and plainspoken man from Vermont, "Silent Cal" was famous for his long silences and short, direct remarks. A man once bet a friend that he could engage Coolidge in a conversation of at least three words. He met Cal and told him of the bet. Coolidge simply replied with *two* words: "You lose." Born on July 4, 1872, Vice President Coolidge became president in 1923, upon the death of President Warren G. Harding. Cal was then elected in 1924 on the slogan, "Keep Cool with Coolidge." Things, however, began to heat up by the end of the 1920s. But fortunately for Coolidge, he was no longer in office when the Great Depression began in 1929. Today, some experts think that his pro-business policies were partly responsible for this event. Perhaps. But terse-talking Cal, who died in 1933, would probably just answer with another Coolidgism: "When a great many people are unable to find work," he once said, "unemployment results."

> "I know not
> what course
> others may take;
> but as for me,
> give me liberty or
> give me death."

At various times in history someone will come out with a brief but immortal phrase. So it is with these words of Patrick Henry, delivered to his fellow Virginians on the eve of the Revolutionary War. But who was Patrick Henry? A self-made man with little schooling, young Henry was elected to the Virginia House of Burgesses in 1765. He soon became well known for his powerful speeches. Many of them called on the colonists to revolt against the mother country, Great Britain. At this time, Henry was a fiery patriot: "I am not a Virginian," he declared, "but an American." His tune changed, however, after the colonies won their freedom. As governor of Virginia, Henry argued for a whole month against the new American Constitution. But this time he was on the losing side. Virginians approved the Constitution and Pat was sent packing. His call for freedom, however, still echoes down to the present time.

"I have a dream."

Martin Luther King's dream was a simple one: that all Americans "will one day live in a nation where they will not be judged by the color of their skin—but by the content of their character." Born in Atlanta, Georgia, in 1929, King was a Christian minister who led the fight for equal justice for black people. But King fought in a very unusual way. He believed in nonviolence. Again and again, he and his supporters—African-Americans and whites—marched, picketed, or entered stores that refused to serve blacks. Often they were met by jeering crowds, bottle-throwing mobs, or police with clubs, water hoses, or vicious dogs. King's response, however, was always the same: stand for what you believe—but don't hurt back. From the South to the North, King carried his message. In many places, laws were changed, giving African-Americans some of their rights. In 1963, over 250,000 people of all races traveled to Washington, D.C., for a huge rally in support of King's movement. His "I Have a Dream" speech was delivered there. A year later, he received the Nobel Peace Prize. When he was assassinated in 1968, Martin Luther King, Jr., was one of the most admired and loved (and by some, the most hated) men in the world.

And what about his dream? It lives on, but in many parts of America it is still more a dream than a waking reality.

"If particular care and attention is not paid to the Ladies we are determined to foment a Rebellion, and will not hold ourselves bound by any Laws in which we have no voice, or Representation"

This is Abigail Adams, reminding her husband, John, to put women's rights on the agenda of the drafting committee of the Declaration of Independence in 1776. (He didn't, but Abigail didn't quit either. She later said to her husband: "We have too many high-sounding words, and too few actions that correspond with them.") Like most women of her time, Abigail received little formal schooling. But she was still one of the keenest observers of life in the American colonies. Many of her thoughts are contained in letters she wrote to friends and relatives. The letters were published in 1840, long after Abigail's death. An outspoken opponent of slavery, she was also a great American patriot. During the Revolutionary War, she watched the British troops in Boston. She then wrote to George Washington to help him make his war plans. The Adams family has a large place in American history. Abigail's husband became president (1797–1801). In 1825, their son, John Quincy Adams, became president, too!

"Men their rights and nothing more; women their rights and nothing less."

Susan B. Anthony and Elizabeth Cady Stanton were the one-two punch for women's rights in nineteenth-century America. At that time, many women could not own property, many could not get jobs, and none could vote. This phrase appeared on the front page of the duo's weekly journal, *The Revolution,* published in the late 1860s. The two editors (and their many friends) called for equal rights for women: equal salaries, equal rights in marriage, and equal voting privileges. Both women lived long lives and devoted them to many causes, including the abolition of slavery. Anthony was a fiery speaker who drew large—and sometimes very angry—crowds. Stanton worked behind the scenes, helping to decide what they would do next. Both women died before one of their major goals, the Nineteenth Amendment, was achieved. This amendment, passed in 1919, finally gave American women the right to vote. Anthony's face appears on the silver dollar. But if she could speak from the grave, she would be more pleased if the motto of *The Revolution* someday came to be the way things are.

"I've never been lost; but I was bewildered once for three days."

If Daniel Boone never got lost, there's not much excuse for us modern city dwellers! A pioneer and woodsman from his teens, Dan roamed over the Appalachian Mountains and led the way into densely wooded Kentucky. While opening up new trails, he had numerous hair-raising adventures. He was even adopted by the Shawnee (a Native American nation). In the midst of many narrow escapes, he still had time to buy over 100,000 Kentucky acres. But after Boone lost title to his "Kentuck" land—after all, it *was* a rather big chunk for one person!—he packed up in 1799 and trekked off to still more distant Missouri, where he continued to hunt and roam until his death in 1820 at age eighty-five—an explorer to the very end.

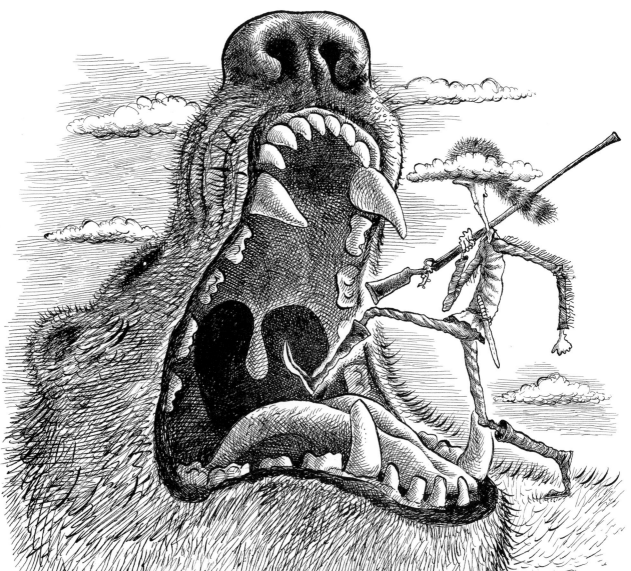

"Are we to give up our ancestors' sacred graves to be plowed for corn?"

Red Cloud answered his own angry question: "Dakotas," he said to his tribespeople, "I am for war." A meteor had fallen on the day of his birth, giving him the name Red Cloud. And Red Cloud became a meteor himself! Throughout the 1860s, his quick-riding warriors bothered and battled the westward-trekking settlers and the United States Army, too. Gold had been discovered in Montana, but the Native Americans blocked the trail. Even when army forts were built, Red Cloud and his men still kept the trail closed. No one knew this part of the West as well as the Indians. (After all, it was their country.) Hard as they tried, the army troops could not outwit their enemy. One of the great military leaders in American history, Red Cloud finally made peace with the American government. But only after the government promised—and followed through on its promise—to leave the forts. Often the United States government did not live up to its promises to the Indians. This is one of the few times Native Americans forced the government to live up to one of its own treaties. Red Cloud had made his point. Later he counseled peace between the whites and the Indians. He lived until 1909, when he died at age eighty-seven in South Dakota.

"Ain't I a woman?"

Yes, she was—and quite a woman indeed. *To sojourn* means to travel, and ex-slave Sojourner Truth did just that, crossing the borders between states and the borders between different kinds of people in pre–Civil War America. After a religious conversion in the 1840s, the six-foot-tall Sojourner set out on foot to preach to the people. She traveled all across the North, protesting against slavery and speaking for oppressed people everywhere, especially women. The fact that Sojourner was an ex-slave and a black woman did not keep her from speaking her mind freely and powerfully. This quote is taken from a famous speech delivered in 1851. She answered a man who claimed that women were too weak to deserve the same rights as men by saying: "I could work as much as a man . . . and ain't I a woman? I have plowed and planted . . . and ain't I a woman? I have borne the lash . . . and ain't I a woman?" Indeed, Sojourner's long journey in pursuit of truth and freedom for all people never ended. She helped African-American soldiers during the Civil War. She even started a "sit-in" protest against segregated streetcars in Washington, D.C. "It is hard for the old slaveholding spirit to die," she said at that time, "but die it must." Later, she urged African-Americans to write letters to Congress demanding freedom for blacks. "Send tons of paper to Washington for the spouters to chaw on," she told her followers. When she died in Battle Creek, Michigan, in 1883, at the age of eighty-six, her funeral and burial drew a record crowd who paid tribute to a great American.

"The only thing we have to fear is fear itself."

"You must do the thing you think you cannot do."

You might call them the "fearless couple." When Franklin Delano Roosevelt was elected president in 1932, there were tough times in America. Millions of workers had lost their jobs, banks were closing, and people were losing their money and their homes. But FDR (President Roosevelt's initials) had already come through fearful times himself. Stricken with polio in 1921 (at age thirty-nine), he struggled back—on paralyzed legs—to become governor of New York and then president of the United States. His program for solving America's problems was called the "New Deal." (The first sentence quoted above was part of his first inaugural address.) Through the hard times of the Depression and through most of World War II, his confident leadership provided much-needed hope during difficult years.

At the same time, Franklin's wife, Eleanor (the author of the second quote), was taking bold steps of her own. Extremely shy as a young woman, Eleanor pushed herself into doing what she never thought she could do: going out among people, speaking up, and taking a stand on important issues. Along the way, she created a new role for presidents' wives. Previous first ladies had mostly given polite teas and shown up at state dinners. But Eleanor talked about serious things. She wrote newspaper columns, held press conferences (often for women reporters only), and worked with young people. She became a powerful voice calling for equality for all Americans. After Franklin's death in 1945, Eleanor kept working. She also helped draft the Declaration of Human Rights for the newly formed United Nations.

"Simplicity, simplicity, simplicity!"

That was Henry David Thoreau's motto—and he wasn't kidding. Can you imagine choosing to live in a small hut with a bare floor and a few simple pieces of furniture? Well, that's what Thoreau did, spending just 28.12^1/_2$ for the things he needed to build his little house. In his famous book *Walden*, he tells about his two years of living, thinking, and writing at Walden Pond, close to the woods and water that he loved. He wrote his book to remind his fellow Americans that they paid far too much attention to small, unimportant details. Thoreau thought that owning too many things kept a person from being free. Take owning a house, for example. "Sometimes a man doesn't own a house," he wrote, "but the house owns the man." Thoreau was an enemy of slavery, too. While he was alive, most people didn't know who he was. But his life and writings have influenced many world leaders such as Mahatma Gandhi and Martin Luther King, Jr., proving that a little (simple) bit goes a long, long way.

"I swing big, and I live big."

Babe Ruth's appetite for hitting home runs was only equaled by his appetite for living. On the field, George Herman "Babe" Ruth, Jr. (also known as "The Sultan of Swat," "The Goliath of Grand Slam," and "The Prince of Pounders") smashed out more four-baggers in some seasons than entire teams. The "Bambino" (yet another nickname) stopped playing in 1935, at age forty. At that time, he had hit more than twice as many homers as any other player in baseball. He had also developed a stomach to match, built up over the years by eating everything in sight. (Perhaps he was making up for the lean years he had spent as a youth in a boys' home.) Anyway, his wild and crazy lifestyle of raccoon coats, sports cars, all-night parties, and a gruff-voiced "Hi, kid" to everyone he met, made him the toast of the Roaring Twenties. Even at his death in 1948, he was still one of the most popular sports heroes in America.

"Genius is one percent inspiration and ninety-nine percent perspiration."

Did he work hard? You might say that Thomas Alva Edison worked so hard that he worked his way right into your house! Indeed, you probably can't go a day without using something that Edison invented or at least improved upon. From electric lights to wax paper, and from the telephone to a flashlight battery, Al (that was his boyhood name) Edison had a hand or a brain in it. All in all, he received a record number of inven-

tion patents from the American government: 1,093, to be exact. Edison started young and kept going for a long time. What "turned him on" the most was electricity. Because he wanted to be a great inventor, Edison built the first ever "invention factory." In this building—which today we would call a research lab—he and his hard-working assistants kept turning things out. His most popular invention was probably the electric light bulb. This invention completely changed American homes. Edison even built the world's first motion picture studio—not in California but in New Jersey. Here he produced the first film ever to tell a story, *The Great Train Robbery.* This early silent movie ran for all of eight minutes way back in 1903. To the end, Edison claimed that his success was caused by nothing more than plain hard work. Whatever it was, he brought many gifts to the world. On the night of his funeral, October 21, 1931, lights were dimmed in all the homes in America—in honor of the genius who just worked and worked and worked.

"Don't trust anyone over thirty."

Those are the words of Jack Weinberg, spoken in 1964. But they might be the motto for one of the most unusual times in American history: the 1960s. Weinberg (born in 1940) was among the millions of young people who changed their ideas, their ways of living, and their country's history in just a few years. This quote came when Weinberg and others were students at the University of California at Berkeley. Many of these students became "Hippies" (long hair, bare feet, the simple life, rock music, and so forth). Others became Yippies, followers of the Youth International Party founded by Jerry Rubin and Abbie Hoffman. (The party had no actual membership, but details like that never much bothered showmen like Jerry and Abbie.) The Yippie program called for America to stop fighting in the Vietnam War. But it also included everything from releasing greased pigs at a presidential inauguration to abolishing pay toilets! Young radicals like Weinberg, Hoffman, and Rubin led or took part in many antiwar protests. The most famous took place in Chicago in 1968, where hundreds of policemen attacked the demonstrators. But time marches on. (One of the popular songs of the period was folk-rocker Bob Dylan's "The Times They Are A-Changin'.") What do you do if *you* live past thirty? Weinberg went on to help people get better working conditions and a better environment. But others took a very different path. When Rubin resurfaced some years later he had become—believe it or not—a successful stockbroker. How now, Jerry? Never trust anyone under *fifty*?

"In the future, everyone will be world-famous for fifteen minutes."

You may someday get *your* fifteen minutes, but artist Andy Warhol—the author of this quote—did quite a bit better than that. From the early 1960s to his death in 1987, Warhol was one of the most famous artists in the world. "I want to be a machine," Andy once proclaimed. And his art often looked just like that—machine made. He even called his art studio "The Factory." His pictures of soup cans, pop bottles, and especially movie stars are examples of an art movement called Pop Art. Pop artists painted common, everyday subjects (that is, popular—"pop"—subjects.) But Andy didn't just make paintings. When not creating art, his cool, ghostly face could be found among the famous and the wanna-be-famous at many of New York City's night clubs. He also made movies. Here, too, he often dealt with everyday subjects in strange ways. In one Warhol film, *Sleep,* the camera remains fixed on a sleeping person for several hours! (Yawn, yawn, yawn.) Was Andy Warhol a great artist? Or was he merely a great self-promoter? Time will tell. But did he get his fifteen-minute fame allotment? No question about it. He got that and a lot more.

"I've been on calendars—but I've never been on time."

True on both counts! Marilyn Monroe was no doubt the most photographed movie actress of the 1950s. Her face—and figure—appeared in countless magazines and newspapers, as well as on many calendars. During her career, however, she was more and more likely to arrive late or delay movie shoots for hours. (Her witty quote, therefore, is playing on two meanings of time: calendar time and hours in the work day.) Once she took nearly a whole day applying makeup and trying different clothing styles to find exactly the right look. Movie directors complained and fumed, but they liked what they got. Serious, funny, and sexy, Marilyn appeared in twenty-eight films (*Niagara, Some Like It Hot,* to name a few) during her short period of stardom. Since her death in 1962 at the age of thirty-six, she has become one of the most written-about film stars in history.

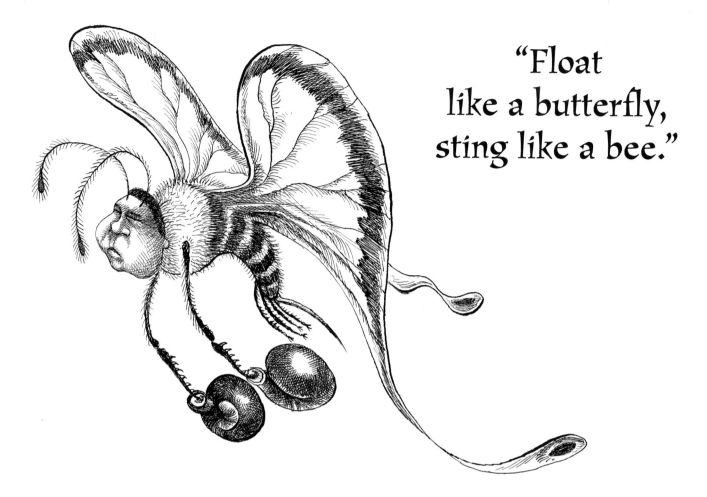

"Float like a butterfly, sting like a bee."

Muhammad Ali said it, and the many boxers he defeated during his long career would agree that he both floated and stung. (Ali was born with the name Cassius Marcellus Clay in 1942, but he changed his name when he converted to the Nation of Islam.) This great boxer first won an Olympic Gold Medal in 1960. After that, he went on to win the world heavyweight title four times: in 1964 at age twenty-two, again in 1967, again in 1974, and finally in 1978. He had the title taken from him once because he refused—for religious reasons—to enter the army during the Vietnam War. "I ain't got no quarrel with the Vietcong," Muhammed explained. Ali's boxing style combined great speed (floating) with sharp punches (stinging). When he needed it, he had a strong knockout punch, too. Sting, sting, bang! One of the most popular and free-spirited figures in sports history, Muhammad liked to make up verses about his fighting ability. Sometimes "The Greatest"—as he liked to call himself—even predicted the round in which he would knock out his opponent.

Starting in the 1920s, Martha Graham brought a new look to modern dance. Her way of dancing was very different from the flowing style of ballet. Ballet featured cool, calm beauty, but Graham's dances expressed strong feelings. Her stage sets, or backgrounds, were different, too. Sometimes, in fact, the sets were very bare: merely black or white walls. This made the dancers stand out clearly as they moved back and forth. Graham created over 150 dance works during her long career. Her dances were often about old myths or Bible stories, but they always showed the thoughts and feelings of the main characters. (That's what she means by the "graph of the heart": the changes in one's thoughts and feelings.) Some of her famous dances are *Heretic,* which deals with the struggle of a rebel against society, and *Primitive Mysteries,* which deals with thoughts about God and religion. Graham loved dancing. Indeed, she loved it so much she kept on going to the very end. When she died in 1991 (at age ninety-seven) she was still working.

"Every dance s a kind of graph of the heart."

"My fellow Americans: Ask not what your country can do for you—ask what you can do for your country."

Almost every American alive at that time can tell you where he or she was on November 22, 1963. President John Fitzgerald Kennedy's death on that day, by an assassin's bullet, stunned the nation. The election of this same president in 1960 brought a new sense of hope to America. At forty-three, JFK was the youngest person ever elected president. This quote is from Kennedy's inaugural address. "Americans," he further said, "would pay any price and meet any hardship to assure the success of liberty." And what could Americans do for their country and for liberty? The few years of Kennedy's shortened term were marked by a powerful movement: to give African-Americans the same liberties that white citizens had. Kennedy tried to pass laws that would allow black Americans to vote and to live anywhere in the United States—just like white Americans. JFK also began the Peace Corps, which sent thousands of Americans to aid the people of poorer countries. More than any one law or program, however, it was Kennedy's youth and energy that made many people support him. He reminded Americans that patriotism on behalf of a good cause was still a noble ideal.

"One had better die fighting against injustice than to die like a rat in a trap."

When the American Civil War ended in 1865, another—less famous—war began in the South. This was the war waged against black people. Although African-Americans were now free, their former owners tried to keep them from owning land, holding jobs, and voting. To keep them from standing up for themselves, white Southerners murdered and lynched hundreds of innocent blacks. (A lynching is the brutal murder of an innocent person by an out-of-control mob.) Born a slave in 1862, Ida B. Wells lived through it all. She began her working life as a schoolteacher, but she was soon fired because she asked for the same books and materials for her black students that white students had. She then became a newspaper editor, where, in her columns, she began to criticize lynching. As a result, her life was threatened. Memphis whites even destroyed the office of her newspaper. Finally Wells moved to the North. Even there, her fight against injustice continued. In the 1890s she published the first book telling about the evils of lynching. She argued that lynchings had nothing to do with justice. Instead, they were being used to keep black people from asking for their rights. Married to a Chicago lawyer, Ida B. Wells-Barnett later helped start a number of groups that aided African-Americans. When she died in 1931, she had long been one of the brightest lights in a very dark chapter of American history.

"I **am** nature."

Can great paintings be made from thin lines of paint zigzagging, whirling, and criss-crossing wildly around and around and back and forth? Well, Jackson Pollock's paintings are just that! With his large, colorful canvases, Pollock helped bring a bold new look to American art. His style was called Abstract Expressionism. Those are big words but they mean something very simple. The paintings are called *abstract* because there are no real-istic images in them. And the word *expressionism* is used because the paintings look as if the artist was trying to show, or express, some inner feeling. Another painter once told Jackson he should paint trees or other scenes from nature. Pollock merely replied with this quote. (In other words, he felt that all the energy of nature was already inside him.) He came to his style slowly, however, after many years of hard work. He liked to spread a huge canvas on the floor and pour, drip, or fling paint on it. Then he would sense, or intuit, which side was up and where to trim the canvas to get the strongest effect. Some critics called his works "action paintings" because they seem to express the action of the painter painting. Pollock lived an active, and sometimes troubled, life, too. He died in a car crash in 1956. But he helped change the way people look at art.

Wow! Emily Dickinson must have felt headless many times! Why? Because she wrote some of the greatest poems ever written in America. Sometimes her poems are about everyday things. One starts like this:

A Bird came down the Walk—
He did not know I saw—
He bit an Angleworm in halves
And ate the fellow, raw.

At other times, her poems were about difficult things, such as what it feels like to die or what we can really know about life. One of these poems starts like this:

Will there really be a "Morning"?
Is there such a thing as "Day"?
Could I see it from the mountains
If I were as tall as they?

She had her own way of writing down her poems. Often she didn't care about titles, and she used dashes in place of commas and periods. But as unusual as many of her poems were, some parts of her life were unusual, too. She always dressed in white. She lived much of her adult life indoors, inside her family home in Amherst, Massachusetts. She had few friends. And she published just ten poems (she wrote over seventeen hundred) during her lifetime. Her sister found all of the poems in a drawer after Emily's death in 1886. People who knew her were amazed to find that shy Emily had left behind tiny, string-tied packets of beautiful poems. So beautiful that they can still make your head lift off. Read one and see for yourself.

"If I feel physically as if the top of my head were taken off, I know that is poetry."

"Anyone who tries to turn back gets a bullet between the eyes!"

Why would anyone say that to someone she was trying to help? When escaped slave Harriet Tubman returned to the South to lead other slaves to freedom, she carried a pistol. If some of the runaways wanted to quit, they got this stern message—or something very much like it—from their Underground Railroad "conductor." Why did Harriet have to act this way? Because she knew that if anyone turned back, all of their lives would be in danger. All in all, Tubman made nineteen rescue missions and led approximately three hundred people to the North. Southern slave owners were so upset that they once placed a $40,000 reward on her head. But Harriet kept doing what she had to do. She even wanted to be with John Brown when he and his men raided Harpers Ferry in an attempt to free the slaves. During the 1860s, Harriet served as a nurse and a Northern spy in the Civil War. She then helped build schools for blacks. And she later started a famous nursing home, also for African-Americans. She was over ninety years old when she died in 1913. But long before that, she had earned the name of Black Moses.

"War is Hell!"

Take it from William Tecumseh Sherman—he went through it all! A leading Northern general in the Civil War, Sherman fought in many battles throughout the South. After a difficult battle, his troops captured the important city of Atlanta in 1864. Following this, Sherman led his army across Georgia. His troops stretched 60 miles wide. They marched through the state, taking or destroying everything of value on their way: food, farms, cattle, forests, and whatever armed forces that tried to stop them. It wasn't very nice, but as Sherman himself admitted, war never is. Most historians think that Sherman's "march to the sea" was one of the main reasons the war ended. Sherman was famous for saying what he meant in a very direct way. Years later the Republican Party asked him to run for president. He sent back this message: "I will not accept if nominated and I will not serve if elected." You might say that means no!

Someone once asked Louis Armstrong: "What is jazz?" This quote is his brief and to-the-point reply. Louis Armstrong was one person who didn't have to ask what jazz is! A cornet and trumpet player from age fourteen (when he learned in a New Orleans boys' home), Armstrong knew that jazz comes from the heart and soul. At least his surely did! "Satchmo" (short for "Satchelmouth," which some people say came from his wide grin) made jazz more popular with his rough, happy-go-lucky singing voice. He was also one of the first jazz musicians to step out in front of his band and perform solos, that is, to play alone. Besides thousands of concert and club shows, he made more than fifteen hundred recordings. These include early records such as *Potato Head Blues* and *Struttin' with Some Barbecue*, along with later vocal hits such as "What a Wonderful World" and "Hello, Dolly." When he died in 1971, he was the most well-known jazz musician in the world. Listen to some of his music and you'll understand why.

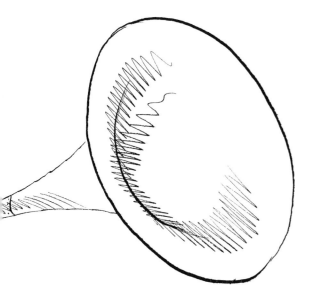

"Man, if you have to ask,
you'll never know."

"Now I have something I can give to everyone."

When Abraham Lincoln was president, hundreds of people would visit the White House each day. Poor Abe had to listen to people who wanted jobs, wanted money, or just wanted to shake the president's hand. When he came down with a mild case of smallpox in 1863, he tossed off the above remark to a friend. Since no one was counting, nobody knows for sure how many visitors came away with the disease! Lincoln's sense of humor was famous, but at the same time he was often very sad. Look at photographs taken at the time he became president in 1861 and the last picture taken a few days before he was assassinated in 1865 at age fifty-six. The lines on his face are a map of the lonely hours he lived through while leading the Union during the Civil War.

"What a shame. If you had stolen a railroad, they would have made you a Senator."

Who do you think "Mother" Jones was talking to? She was speaking to a man who had been sentenced to jail for stealing—guess what—one loaf of bread! (This was during a time when some U.S. Senators were famous for taking huge bribes.) With her blunt words, "Mother" Jones voiced the anger of many American workers during her lifetime. Irish-born Mary Harris "Mother" Jones came to America as a young girl. After her husband and children died in a yellow fever epidemic, she spent much of her long life helping workers stand up for their rights. Wearing prim black dresses decked with lace, she looked like the perfect picture of a grandmother. But she didn't sit around in any rocking chair. Once she marched with poor children to the New York home of President Theodore Roosevelt. She wanted to demonstrate that a decent country should take better care of its children. Another time she led the wives of coal miners over the mountains banging on tin pans. Why did she do this? To make people wake up to the fact that miners were being treated unfairly. She went wherever her cause called her. Once she claimed that her only home was "wherever there was a good fight against wrong." For her final home, she asked on her deathbed to be buried with "her boys"—miners killed in southern Illinois. To the very end, she lived by the words she wrote in her autobiography: "Pray for the dead— and fight like hell for the living."

"I don't care to belong to any club that will accept me as a member."

Groucho Marx liked to laugh and to make people laugh with him. He was as ready to poke fun at himself as he was to poke fun at anyone else. And he did just that for over fifty years—in films or onstage or on TV. Groucho usually performed with his equally zany brothers, Chico, Harpo, and Zeppo. Together, they created a comedy team known as the Marx Brothers. Groucho (born Julius Henry Marx in 1890) was the wisecracking, fast-talking brother with the long cigar, bushy mustache, dark, thick eyebrows, and comically rolling eyes. He liked very much to change a word's meaning to make a joke. Example. "I want to marry you—and you," says Groucho, pointing to two women. "That would be bigamy!" one of the women protests. (*Bigamy*, which is illegal in America, is when a person is married to two people at the same time.) "Yes," Groucho answers, "I agree. That would be very *big o' me!*" Among the most popular Marx Brothers movies are *Duck Soup* and *A Night at the Opera*. When Groucho died in 1977, he had a loyal and delighted following. His fans, no doubt, would have paid a good deal to be part of any club to which *he* belonged!

"I look at my work and make up my mind about it. After that, neither flattery nor criticism matters to me."

Becoming a great artist takes good work habits and thick skin—and Georgia O'Keeffe had both. As a young art student in the early 1900s, O'Keeffe was told by a fellow student that she should become a model, not an artist! But she just laughed and went on working. This quote is something she said before one of her many successful art shows. She didn't mean that her paintings were too good to criticize. She meant that she had tried to do her best, and because she had done her best, she was satisfied for the moment. And Georgia O'Keeffe's best was very good indeed. She painted everything from sunsets in Texas, where she taught as a young woman, to skyscrapers in New York, where she lived for several years with her photographer husband, Alfred Stieglitz. She is also well-known for her very large and colorful flower paintings. The last half of her life was lived mostly in New Mexico. Here she found inspiration in the clean white bones of dead animals and the clear outlines of the dry desert landscape.

"Housekeeping ain't no joke."

The writer was Louisa May Alcott. The speaker is the housekeeper, Hannah, in Alcott's famous novel *Little Women*. But the idea was one that the little women of the novel (the four young sisters: Meg, Jo, Beth, and Amy) quickly agreed with. In one part of the novel, the girls are left to themselves to cook dinner and clean their large house. The results are disastrous—they quickly realize that housekeeping is every bit of a full-time job. Truly, it "ain't no joke." Louisa May Alcott lived during a time when women were supposed to marry, have children, and clean the house, period. More than anything else, however, Alcott wanted to become a writer. (Jo in *Little Women* is like Alcott herself, just as the novel is based on her own family.) She worked in an army hospital during the Civil War. Later she wrote a book about what happened to her during the war. Still later, she wrote *Little Women*, which made her famous throughout America. All her best books show that she cared about poor people and women's rights. To Alcott, living a full life meant doing more than just keeping house. She would have agreed with a later writer (Rose Macaulay) who said, "A house unkept cannot be so distressing as a life unlived."